LOST IN NEW YORK

Adapted by Jordan Horowitz
From the screenplay written by John Hughes

SCHOLASTIC INC.
New York Toronto London Auckland Sydney

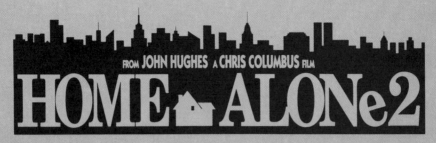

LOST IN NEW YORK

TWENTIETH CENTURY FOX PRESENTS A JOHN HUGHES PRODUCTION A CHRIS COLUMBUS FILM
MACAULAY CULKIN JOE PESCI DANIEL STERN JOHN HEARD HOME ALONE 2 TIM CURRY BRENDA FRICKER
AND CATHERINE O'HARA MUSIC BY JOHN WILLIAMS FILM EDITOR RAJA GOSNELL PRODUCTION DESIGNER SANDY VENEZIANO DIRECTOR OF PHOTOGRAPHY JULIO MACAT
EXECUTIVE PRODUCERS MARK RADCLIFFE DUNCAN HENDERSON RICHARD VANE WRITTEN AND PRODUCED BY JOHN HUGHES DIRECTED BY CHRIS COLUMBUS

HUGHES

DOLBY STEREO
IN SELECTED THEATRES

SOUNDTRACK AVAILABLE ON FOX RECORDS

COLOR BY DELUXE ®

COPYRIGHT © 1992 TWENTIETH CENTURY FOX

ISBN 0-590-45719-5

Book designed by Ursula Herzog

12 11 10 9 8 7 6 5 4 3 2   2 3 4 5 6 7/9

Printed in the U.S.A.   24

First Scholastic printing, November 1992

It was the night of the grade school Christmas pageant. Kevin McCallister and his brother Buzz were going to sing in the children's choir.

Kevin's whole family was there. Uncle Frank and Aunt Leslie were there, too. Everyone was excited because Kevin was going to sing a solo.

Kevin was nervous. He had never performed a solo before. He started to sing. His voice was pleasant and sweet. Everybody liked it.

But Buzz had planned a mean trick. He took electric candles and placed them behind Kevin's ears. As Kevin sang, it looked liked his ears were glowing!

People in the audience began laughing at Kevin. Even Uncle Frank let out a big snort.

"Kevin, I'm sorry," said Buzz when they got home.
But Kevin knew Buzz wasn't sorry.
"Someday I'm going to go away all by myself," Kevin said,
pouting. "Then no one will cause me any trouble."

The next day the McCallisters were going to Florida. They overslept as usual. Everybody was frantic. They had to get to the airport on time.

Kevin remembered last Christmas when his family went on vacation. They had left him behind!

"This time I'll carry my own ticket," he said. "Just in case you guys try and ditch me again."

At the airport Kevin needed batteries to listen to his Talkboy. He looked inside his dad's traveling bag. Next to his batteries were a camera, an address book, magazines, and his dad's wallet. The wallet was filled with money and credit cards.

Kevin saw his father rushing to board the airplane for Florida. "Dad! Wait for me!" shouted Kevin.

He flung the traveling bag over his shoulder and ran after his father. He didn't want to get left behind again.

Kevin listened to his Talkboy during the whole flight. When the plane landed he looked for his father. Instead he found a big surprise.

The man wasn't his father at all. He was just wearing the same coat. From behind, they looked exactly alike.

Next Kevin noticed that all the people in the airport wore winter clothes. He thought that was funny clothing for people to wear in Florida where it is warm all year round.

Then Kevin looked through a window and saw the skyline of a city. There were big skyscrapers made of granite and glass. It didn't exactly look like Florida to him.

"Excuse me," said Kevin when he found a ticket agent. "What city is this?"

"New York," replied the ticket agent.

"Yikes!" gasped Kevin. "I did it again! My family's in Florida and I'm in New York — alone!"

Suddenly Kevin smiled. Now he could have some *real* fun!

The first thing he needed was a place to stay. He decided to check in to a hotel. Getting a room was no problem. He still had his dad's credit card!

A bellman took Kevin to his room. Kevin looked around.

There was a king-size bed. There was a refrigerator stuffed with sodas and snacks. There was even a TV in the bathroom.

"How convenient!" said Kevin.

"Is everything all right, sir?" asked the bellman. "Do you know how the TV works?"

"I'm ten years old," replied Kevin. "TV is my life."

The bellman was holding out his hand waiting for a tip. Kevin gave him the best tip he could think of: a stick of gum!

Next Kevin ordered room service.

First he ordered a stack of scary video movies — the kind his parents would never let him watch.

Then a waiter came up and prepared a huge ice cream sundae right in his room!

"Now *this* is a vacation!" said Kevin happily.

After he had watched a few movies . . . and after he had eaten
a few sundaes . . . Kevin lay in bed looking through his father's
address book. He found the address of his Uncle Rob who lived in
New York.

"If they're back from vacation I'll visit them," he decided. "They
usually give good Christmas presents."

The next day Kevin rode in a luxurious limousine that had its own TV. Kevin sat in the back and ate a whole pizza.

Kevin got out in front of Duncan's Toy Chest. It was the world's largest and grandest toy store. Just thinking about all the toys inside made him smile.

Once inside, Kevin hopped on a trampoline. He jumped up and down. WHEEEEE!

Then he picked out all the toys he wanted to buy. He chose mini-robots, Monster Sap Bath Bubbles, a jackknife, and video games.

"Merry Christmas, Kevin," he told himself.

"You have a really nice store here," Kevin told the checkout man.

"Mr. Duncan loves kids," replied the checkout man. "In fact, all the money the store makes today Mr. Duncan will donate to the Children's Hospital."

Kevin felt guilty that he was spending all his dad's money on toys for himself. He gave the checkout man an extra twenty dollars for the Children's Hospital.

Outside, Kevin waited for the limousine to pick him up. While he waited he played with his jackknife.

"Hiya, pal," he heard a familiar voice say.

Kevin looked up. It was Harry and Marv, the two crooks who had tried to rob his house last Christmas!

"Ahhh!" Kevin screamed. He ran away as fast as he could.

Harry and Marv chased Kevin until they caught up with him outside the hotel.

"Tonight at midnight we're robbin' Duncan's Toy Chest," Marv said. "And this time this kid ain't gonna be around to stop us!"

Kevin knew he had to do something, fast. So he did the first thing he could think of. He punched Harry as hard as he could. Harry fell down. He let go of Kevin.

Kevin ran off.

Harry and Marv chased him all through the city. Kevin finally escaped by running into Central Park. Harry and Marv looked everywhere. But Central Park was too big a place in which to find just one little boy.

As the sun sank behind the skyscrapers Kevin walked around
Central Park. He was frightened and lonely.

"Mom, where are you?" he wondered out loud.

He went to Uncle Rob's address, but nobody was home. They were
still on vacation.

Kevin didn't know where to go. If he went back to the hotel Harry
and Marv would get him. Besides, the streets of the city were scary.
He decided to spend the night in the park.

The only thing he had to eat was a bag of corn chips. A hungry-looking pigeon walked up to him.

"I guess you missed your dinner, too," said Kevin. He broke off a small piece and fed the pigeon.

Soon a whole flock of pigeons walked up to Kevin. "I don't know if I have enough for everybody," Kevin told the hungry birds.

All of a sudden the pigeons flapped their wings and turned away. Kevin looked up. The pigeons had perched themselves on the head and arms of a very old lady.

At first the sight of the strange old pigeon lady frightened Kevin. Then he noticed that the pigeons seemed to like her. She had a pocketful of seeds for them to eat. She was their friend.

The pigeon lady took Kevin to a secret attic in Radio City Music Hall. She wanted Kevin to be safe and warm. Soon she and Kevin had become good friends.

Kevin told his new friend that he had done some bad things. Now he was in trouble.

"A good deed erases a bad deed," said the pigeon lady.

That gave Kevin an idea.

Kevin said good-bye to the pigeon lady. He ran to his Uncle Rob's house as fast as he could.

First, he poured Monster Sap all over the floor.

Then, he loaded a piece of cloth with glue.

Finally, he went up to the roof and made a neat stack of bricks.

When he was all done he hurried over to Duncan's Toy Chest.

Kevin looked through the window of the toy store. He saw Harry and Marv stealing money from the cash register.

"This is it," he told himself. "There's no turning back."

Kevin tapped on the window to get the crooks' attention. They were surprised to see him. Then he took a picture of them stealing money. FLASH!

Harry and Marv chased Kevin right to Uncle Rob's house. "I'm up here," shouted Kevin from the roof. "Come and get me!"

"If you throw down your camera we won't hurt you," promised Harry.

Kevin tricked Harry. Instead of throwing his camera he dropped a brick. WHACK! The brick hit Marv. He fell down.

"Nobody throws bricks at me and gets away with it!" threatened Harry.

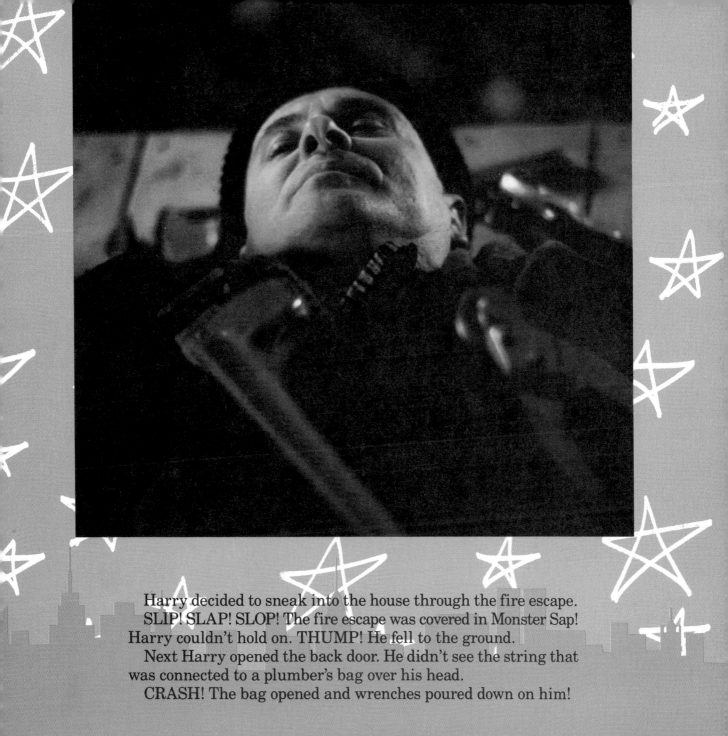

Harry decided to sneak into the house through the fire escape.
SLIP! SLAP! SLOP! The fire escape was covered in Monster Sap!
Harry couldn't hold on. THUMP! He fell to the ground.

Next Harry opened the back door. He didn't see the string that
was connected to a plumber's bag over his head.

CRASH! The bag opened and wrenches poured down on him!

Meanwhile, Marv broke through the front door. Once inside, he looked down. OOPS! There was no floor! FLUMP! Marv fell all the way down to the basement.

He tried to get up, but SLIP! the floor was covered with Monster Sap. SLOP! SLAP! He slipped and slid right into a row of paint cans! The paints made Marv look like a gooey rainbow.

He tugged at a rope, but didn't see that it was connected to a big bag. WOOSH! The bag opened up and covered Marv with plaster.

"Don't you guys know that a kid always wins against two idiots?" taunted Kevin.

Kevin ran outside and called the police.

All of a sudden he felt a pair of cold hands squeezing his neck. It was the crooks!

"Should we bomb him with a sewer pipe?" asked Harry. "Should we throw him in the basement?"

Kevin was scared.

Just then a shower of birdseed rained down on Harry and Marv.
They let go of Kevin and looked up at the sky. A flock of pigeons
swooped down on them!

Kevin looked up, too. Standing behind the two crooks was his
friend, the pigeon lady. She had rescued him.

"This is great," said Kevin as the police arrived and took Harry
and Marv back to jail.

Now Kevin was all alone again. He walked through the streets of New York and stopped at a huge Christmas tree. He wished he could see his family.

"I take back every mean thing I ever said to my family," said Kevin. "I just want my mother."

Then he heard a bell ring in the wind. He turned around. His eyes opened wide in surprise. There was his mother holding a silver Christmas bell!

Kevin's eyes welled with tears as he ran into her arms. "Merry Christmas, sweetheart," she said. They happily hugged and kissed each other.

The next morning Kevin and his whole family woke up to a big surprise.

Mr. Duncan had sent a beautiful Christmas tree and two large chests filled with all kinds of toys to their hotel rooms. It was a reward for Kevin's good deed. Kevin had stopped the crooks. Now the money could be sent to the Children's Hospital where it belonged.

Kevin had helped make all the children's Christmas wishes come true.

This was Kevin's best Christmas ever!